W9-APU-364

Lizard's Escape!

by Trish Kline

Illustrated by Fred Smith

This book is dedicated to my wife, Jackie, whose support and patience has made my illustration career possible — F.S.

© 2002 Trudy Corporation and the Smithsonian Institution, Washington DC 20560.

Published by Soundprints Division of Trudy Corporation, Norwalk, Connecticut.

All rights reserved. No part of this book may be reproduced or transmitted in any form or by any means whatsoever without prior written permission of the publisher.

Book design: Marcin D. Pilchowski
Editor: Laura Gates Galvin
Editorial assistance: Chelsea Shriver

First Edition 2002
10 9 8 7 6 5 4 3 2 1
Printed in China

Acknowledgments:
    Soundprints would like to thank Ellen Nanney and Robyn Bissette at the Smithsonian Institution's Office of Product Development and Licensing for their help in the creation of this book.

*Library of Congress Cataloging-in-Publication Data is
on file with the publisher and the Library of Congress.*

Table of Contents

A note to the reader:
Throughout this story you will see words in **bold letters**. There is more information about these words in the glossary. The glossary is in the back of the book.

Chapter 1
Soaking in the Sun

It is spring. The air is warm. The ground is losing its chill. Prairie Skink has just come out of **hibernation**.

Prairie Skink is a lizard. She has spent the winter in a **burrow**. After a long winter's sleep, she likes to stretch out on a rock in the sunshine.

Even lying on a rock, Prairie Skink is not easy to see! She is brown all over, with a thin white stripe, and wider brown stripes on her sides. From head to tail, Prairie Skink is about seven inches long.

Prairie Skink does not spend all day lying on rocks. The sun warms her and now she can hunt for food. She does not have to go far to find her **prey**.

Prairie Skink lives along dry **streambeds** in open **grasslands**. In the rocks and sand are the kinds of things Prairie Skink likes to eat. There are also things that would like to eat Prairie Skink!

Chapter 2
A Meal!

Prairie Skink begins her search for food. Her body stays very close to the ground. She walks very fast. It looks like she is running!

Prairie Skink looks around rocks and clumps of grass. She finds beetles, spiders and crickets. They are not hard for Prairie Skink to catch.

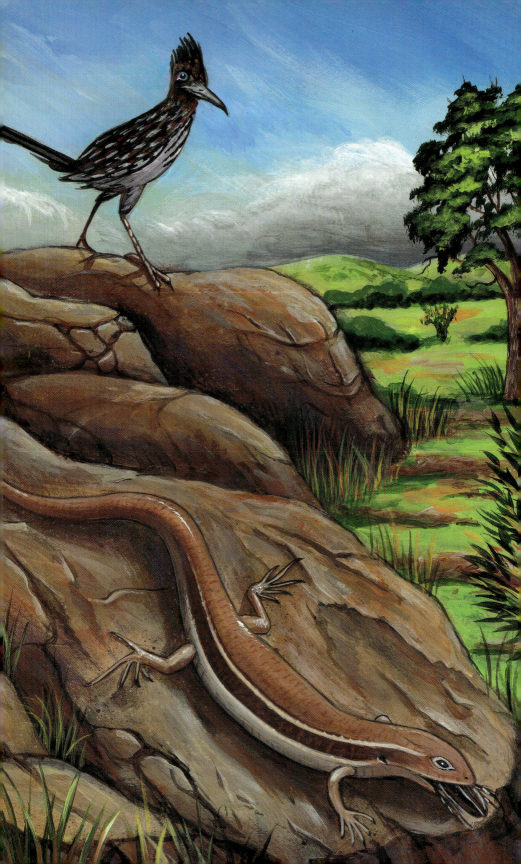

Prairie Skink searches for more food. The sun shines on her back. Her shiny scales catch the attention of a **predator**. Prairie Skink has many predators. Snakes, foxes and hawks often chase her. This time it is a roadrunner.

Prairie Skink doesn't see the roadrunner. The bird has come from behind. By the time she sees him, it is too late! Roadrunner's beak snaps shut on Prairie Skink's long tail.

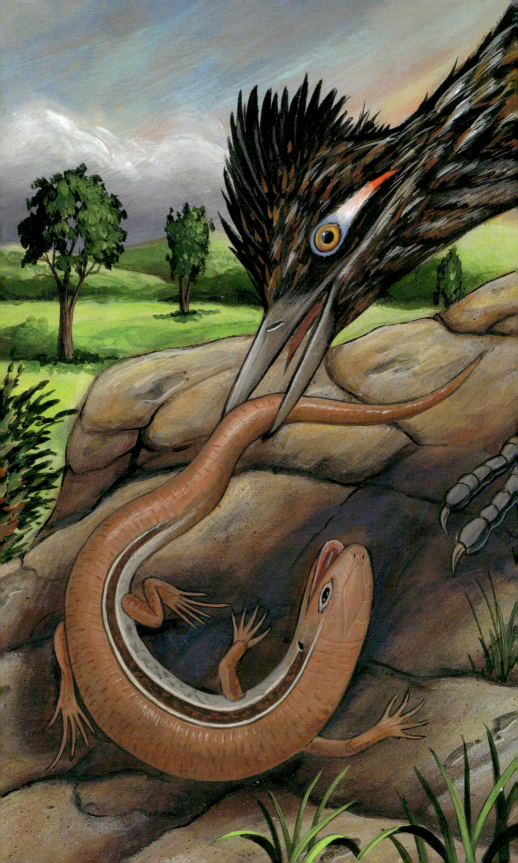

Chapter 3

An Escape!

Prairie Skink tries to run. But she cannot. Roadrunner has her tail. He does not let go. Roadrunner pulls hard. She has to get away! Right now!

Roadrunner lifts Prairie Skink by her tail. To his surprise, the tail breaks! Prairie Skink runs fast. She slips beneath a rock.

Roadrunner is hungry.

He scratches at the rock.

But Prairie Skink is

safe. She has escaped.

Roadrunner will have

to look somewhere else

for his lunch.

Prairie Skink can make her tail fall off! Using this trick helps her to escape from predators. Some animals have claws. Some have sharp teeth. Others have shells. Prairie Skink has a tail that falls off.

Prairie Skink sits under the rock. She looks at her broken tail. She knows it will grow back soon. She will have to be very careful until it does.

Chapter 4

Getting Ready

It is a warm June morning. Prairie Skink is going to lay eggs soon. She must find a special place to lay her eggs.

Prairie Skink looks under a rock. But it is not safe enough for her eggs. She looks beneath a log. It is warm, but not hot. The dirt is soft. It will keep Prairie Skink and her eggs safe. This is the right place.

Prairie Skink lays her eggs in the soft dirt. She has eight small, white eggs. Prairie Skink stays with her eggs. She only leaves them to hunt for food.

After five weeks, the eggs begin to hatch. The hatchling skinks have bright blue tails. Almost immediately, they leave the nest. They begin to hunt for their own food. They do not return to the nest.

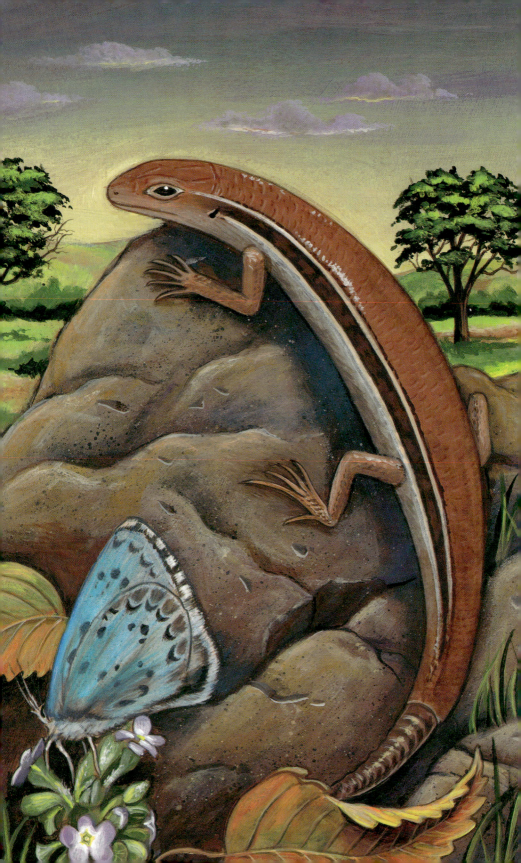

Prairie Skink is alone for the rest of the summer. She suns on a rock. She hunts for food. In winter, Prairie Skink will hibernate again. When spring comes, Prairie Skink will be back in the sunshine. But it may not be easy to spot her!

Glossary

Burrow: a hole or tunnel dug in the ground by an animal.

Grassland: a grassy plot of land.

Hibernation: a sleep-like condition.

Predator: an animal that hunts other animals.

Prey: an animal hunted for food.

Streambed: an area that contains, or once contained, a stream.

Wilderness Facts
About the Prairie Skink

Prairie skinks are grassland lizards. They live among thick clumps of grass, under old boards and other pieces of collapsed homesteads.

Prairie skinks sometimes prefer to lie under covered areas than to be out in the open. Though they have to go out to search for their food, occasionally they get lucky and food, like a cricket, crawls near them.

Prairie skinks can drop part of their tails to escape predators. Usually the new tail is shorter. All young prairie skinks hatch with bright blue tails. Adult male prairie skinks' tails remain blue, but the brightness fades as they get older. Adult female prairie skinks are tan or brown with stripes.

Animals that live near prairie skinks on the prairie include:

Jackrabbits	Western kingbirds
Prairie dogs	Swainson's hawks
Roadrunners	Rattlesnakes
Hispid pocket mice	Coyotes